Presented to

_____

With love from

_____

On

_____

To Perry and Caroline: Thanks for convincing me that two puppies are better than one.
Life wouldn't be nearly as fun without our two very wild but very good dogs.
–M. S.

For my best friend Meg ... the fastest runner, the stealer of socks,
the chaser of birds. The sneakiest dog.
–L. W.

ZONDERKIDZ

Piper & Mabel
Copyright © 2020 by Melanie Shankle
Illustrations © 2020 by Laura Watkins

Requests for information should be addressed to:

Zonderkidz, 3900 Sparks Drive SE, Grand Rapids, Michigan 49546

Library of Congress Cataloging-in-Publication Data

Names: Shankle, Melanie, author. | Watkins, Laura, illustrator.
Title: Piper and Mabel : two very wild but very good dogs / by Melanie
  Shankle ; illustrated by Laura Watkins.
Description: Grand Rapids, Michigan : Zonderkidz, [2020] | Summary: When
  their family takes a beach vacation, Piper and Mabel are left at the Happy
  Tails Ranch, but run away after seeing it is not a real ranch. |
  Identifiers: LCCN 2019012746 (print) | LCCN 2019018032 (ebook) | ISBN
  9780310760870 () | ISBN 9780310760863 (hardback)
Subjects: | CYAC: Dogs--Fiction. | Vacations--Fiction.
Classification: LCC PZ7.1.S4825 (ebook) | LCC PZ7.1.S4825 Pip 2020 (print) |
  DDC [E]–dc23
LC record available at https://lccn.loc.gov/2019012746

Art Direction and Design: Cindy Davis

Printed in China

19 20 21 22 23 /DSC / 19 18 17 16 15 14 13 12 11 10 9 8 7 6 5 4 3 2 1

Piper & Mabel

Two Very Wild but Very Good Dogs

Written by Melanie Shankle   Illustrated by Laura Watkins

ZONDERkidz

Piper and Mabel are two very wild but very good dogs.
They love their people, they love their food,

and they love the cozy, warm beds
where they curl up every night.

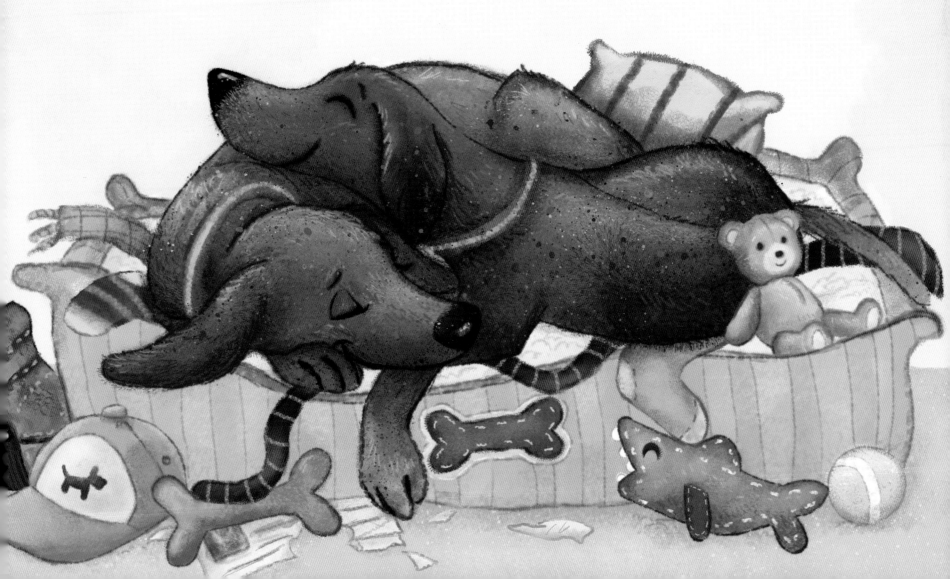

But what they love most of all is adventure.

That's why Piper and Mabel were so excited when they saw their people packing for a vacation.

"Piper! I think we're going to a place called the beach!" barked Mabel.

"The beach sounds delicious!" Piper replied.

Two very wild but very good dogs love nothing more than to feel the wind in their ears as they set off for new and fun places. So a trip to the beach sounds like just the ticket!

"Sorry, but you can't come to the beach with us. You two are going to spend the week at Happy Tails Ranch!"

"Wait a minute! Why aren't we going to the beach with our people?" Mabel asked. "What's the Happy Tails Ranch?!"

"I don't know!" Piper barked. "But it sure sounds happy!"

"Maybe there will be rabbits to chase and creeks to swim in and all kinds of delicious-smelling things to roll in! I bet they'll even grill steaks for us!"

Mabel still wasn't sure. "I don't know about this.
I think I'd rather be with our people at the beach ...
but maybe it will be okay."

"It will be great, Mabel! We can run after cows and dig great big holes!"

So Piper and Mabel began to dream of all the wonderful things they would get to do during their stay at the Happy Tails Ranch.

Mabel started feeling better about Happy Tails Ranch,
so she took out her notebook and wrote a poem called a haiku:

Sister says it's fun
Maybe I'll get a facial
We'll see how it goes

The big day finally arrived!

Piper and Mabel couldn't wait to get through the gates of Happy Tails Ranch. The friendly manager petted them both on the head and gave them doggy treats as she sang out to their people, "No news is good news! We'll call you if there's a problem, but I'm sure Piper and Mabel will have a great time here at Happy Tails Ranch!"

"Did you hear that, Mabel?" asked Piper. "We're going to have a great time! I think I already smell lunch!"

The two very wild but very good dogs licked their people goodbye and let the nice ranch manager lead them through the gates, where they were certain big fun was waiting.

"This isn't a ranch! This is just a big yard! Where are the bunnies to chase? Where is the creek to swim in?" Piper whined.

"We've been tricked!" barked Mabel. "There's no cowboy hat for me to wear! And where's the spa? C'mon, Piper, let's make a run for it!"

And with that, Mabel and Piper tried their hardest to jump over the fence—because two very wild but very good dogs don't want to be away from their people if they can't be at a *real* ranch.

They jumped and they jumped and they jumped until they leapt right over the fence.

Piper and Mabel dashed through the parking lot, slid through a mud puddle, and ran and ran until they realized they were never going to find their people or their way back home.

And then they realized something else.

They were lost.

Piper and Mabel looked around and discovered they couldn't see Happy Tails Ranch anymore. In fact, they couldn't see anything that looked familiar.

They walked around, trying to find their way back. "We're going in circles!" barked Piper.

Mabel began to worry, so she pulled out her notebook and wrote a haiku:

Lost and so alone
I shouldn't have jumped that fence
Regret tastes bitter

Piper's stomach started to growl. "I'm starving!" she said. So Piper began to use her nose to find something to eat, because a very wild but very good dog is still hungry even when she's lost.

"Do you smell anything?" asked Mabel. "It's getting late and I'm afraid!"

"I smell doggy treats!"
barked Piper.

Mabel thought Piper was imagining things, but
she followed her anyway. After sniffing out an old
sandwich, a rotten apple, and a smelly sock, Piper's
nose led them straight to those doggy treats ...

... and the Happy Tails Ranch manager.

"Piper! Mabel! Come here, you very wild but very good dogs!" They ran toward her as fast as they could. They knew she would take them back where they belonged.

She also called their people and told them about Piper and Mabel's big adventure. "I'm just not sure Happy Tails Ranch is the place for two very wild but very good dogs," suggested the manager.

And that's how Piper and Mabel found themselves
on the very best vacation of all ...

With their people at the beach!

Right before they went to sleep that night,
Mabel wrote one last haiku for the day:

Did not like that ranch
No hat, boots, or jingly spurs
No good treats like s'mores

Then Mabel turned to Piper and asked, "What will you remember most about today?"

Piper thought for just a second and replied, "Dinner."

Mabel said, "I will remember those umbrella drinks and that sandcastle we built."

Then the two very wild but very good dogs closed their eyes and said a goodnight prayer:

"Thank you, God, for this day. And thank you for the beach, our people, and most of all for keeping us safe. We promise we will always do our best and never run away."

"... Unless they leave us at Happy Tails Ranch again.
Amen."